RAINBOW magic ®

The Pet Keeper Fairies

For Leandro D'Olivera with my love

Special thanks to
Sue Mongredien

ORCHARD BOOKS
338 Euston Road, London NW1 3BH
Hachette Children's Books
Orchard Books Australia
Level 17/207 Kent Street, Sydney, NSW 2000
A Paperback Original

First published in Great Britain in 2006
Rainbow Magic is a registered trademark of Working Partners Limited.
Series created by Working Partners Limited, London W6 OQT

Text © Working Partners Limited 2006
Illustrations © Georgie Ripper 2006
The right of Georgie Ripper to be identified as the illustrator
of this work has been asserted by her in accordance
with the Copyright, Designs and Patents Act, 1988.
A CIP catalogue record for this book is available
from the British Library.

ISBN 1 84616 167 3
1 3 5 7 9 10 8 6 4 2

Printed and bound in China

Harriet the Hamster Fairy

by Daisy Meadows

illustrated by Georgie Ripper

ORCHARD BOOKS

www.rainbowmagic.co.uk

Fairies with their pets I see
And yet no pet has chosen me!
So I will get some of my own
To share my perfect frosty home.

This spell I cast. Its aim is clear:
To bring the magic pets straight here.
Pet Keeper Fairies soon will see
Their seven pets living with me!

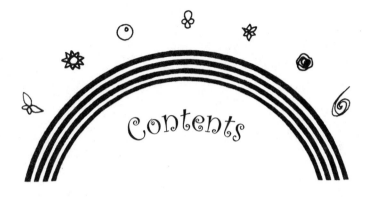

Contents

Hamster-sitting

"Here we go," Kirsty Tate said to her best friend, Rachel Walker, turning the key in the back door of her neighbours' house. "Nibbles! Time for breakfast!" she called, as the door swung open. "Just wait until you see him," she said to Rachel with a grin. "He's adorable. I love hamster-sitting!"

Kirsty's neighbour, Jamie Cooper, had asked Kirsty to feed Nibbles, his little orange and white hamster, while he and his parents were away. She had said yes immediately.

"We just need to top up his food and water," Kirsty told Rachel. "And if we're lucky, he might eat his sunflower seeds out of our hands!"

"How sweet!" Rachel said. "Where's his cage?"

"Over here," Kirsty replied, heading into the lounge.

An excited feeling bubbled up inside Rachel as she followed her friend. This was another pet that they were going to see, after all, and over the last few days, she and Kirsty had had some very exciting pet adventures!

Rachel was staying with Kirsty's family for a whole week, and on the very first day of her holiday, the two girls had met the Pet Keeper Fairies of Fairyland! The fairies had asked Rachel and Kirsty for their help. Jack Frost had wanted a pet of his own, but in Fairyland, pets choose their owners and none of them had chosen Jack Frost. He had been so annoyed by this that he had stolen the Pet Keeper Fairies' magical pets for himself! Luckily, the pets had all escaped from Jack Frost into the human world, but that meant that now they were wandering around lost!

Rachel and Kirsty were helping the Pet Keeper Fairies find the magic pets before Jack Frost's mean goblin servants did. So far, the girls had found four: Shimmer the kitten, Misty the bunny, Sparky the guinea pig and Sunny the puppy. But there were still three pets missing.

Kirsty led Rachel across the lounge to the side table where Nibbles' cage stood. But when the girls arrived, they saw at once that something was wrong: the cage door was wide open!

"Oh, no!" Kirsty cried. "Don't tell me that Nibbles has managed to escape on

my very first day of looking after him!"
She carefully put her hand into the
cage and searched through the wood
shavings and newspaper shreds for the
little hamster, but it was too late. The
cage was empty.

She and Rachel began searching everywhere they could think of in the lounge. They looked under the table, around all the chairs and behind the television. But there was no sign of Jamie's hamster.

"Nibbles!" Rachel called, picking up his food bowl and rattling it. "Nibbles, come and have something to eat."

"Jamie's going to be so upset if he comes home and Nibbles is missing," Kirsty said, anxiously. "Nibbles! Where are you?"

"He could be absolutely anywhere in the house," Rachel said. "Come on, let's try another room."

Kirsty nodded and the girls headed out of the lounge. But just as they reached the door, Kirsty spotted something. "Rachel, look!" she cried, bending down to examine the carpet.

She picked up a stray wood shaving and held it up triumphantly. "A clue!"

"It must have been stuck to one of Nibbles' feet when he climbed out of the cage," Rachel guessed. "Look, there's another by the doorway. And another!"

The two girls followed the trail of wood shavings out into the hall and began searching around the coat rack and the telephone table.

Kirsty picked up the
morning post from
the doormat and
noticed that some
of the envelopes
were a little
shredded. "Look!"
she exclaimed.
"Someone's been
tearing the post!"
Then she smiled as
she realised what had
happened. "Hamsters shred
paper to make nests, don't they?" she
added. "I think Nibbles must have
started trying to make a nest here!" She
giggled as she put the letters on the
table, safely out of reach. "Where did
he go next, I wonder?"

"This way," Rachel said, spotting
a couple of pieces of shredded paper
near the kitchen. "Come on!"

In the kitchen, the girls peered under
the table and chairs, but there was no
sign of a small, furry hamster.

"Someone's been nibbling this fruit,"

Kirsty said, picking up
an apple from the fruit
bowl. Tiny teeth had
punctured the skin
in several places.

"Nibbles must
have stopped for
a snack." Then she
frowned. "How on
earth did he get up
onto the kitchen
counter, though?"

Rachel pointed at the nearby curtain. "Hamsters have strong claws," she pointed out. "I expect Nibbles climbed up the curtain to reach the counter top." She grinned, imagining the scene. "Nibbles is very clever, isn't he?"

"Yes," Kirsty agreed, scanning the kitchen and the curtains, hoping to spot a flash of orange and white fur. "But he's not here any more. We'd better keep looking."

Rachel suddenly froze on the spot. "Sssh!" she whispered to Kirsty, putting a finger to her lips. "What's that noise?"

Both girls stood still and listened hard. They could just hear a faint scratching sound coming from the hallway.

Kirsty grinned at Rachel. "Phew! It must be Nibbles scratching," she said. "All we need to do is follow that sound, and it should lead us straight to one very adventurous hamster!"

The girls tiptoed out of the kitchen in the direction of the scratching noise. The sound seemed to be getting louder as they approached the cupboard under the stairs.

"Nibbles, I'm coming to get you!"
Kirsty giggled. She stepped forwards to
open the cupboard door, but before she
could quite reach it, the door swung
open by itself – and out jumped one of
Jack Frost's horrible green goblins!

Harriet Drops In

"Oh!" gasped Kirsty, as the goblin laughed rudely, charged out of the cupboard and ran up the stairs.

Before either girl could say a word, a second goblin stuck his head over the banisters and cheekily blew raspberries at them!

Kirsty and Rachel looked at each other.

Goblins in the Coopers' house could mean only one thing!

"There must be a fairy pet nearby," Rachel whispered, her heart thumping.

"Yes, and we've got to find it before the goblins do!" Kirsty agreed, her eyes darting everywhere.

"Go away!" came a rude shout from upstairs.

Rachel and Kirsty both looked up to see that there were now three goblins peering over the banisters.

"We won't go away," Kirsty said, putting her hands on her hips. "We've come to feed Jamie's hamster. We're supposed to be here!"

The goblins all burst out laughing. "Hamster gone missing, has he?" one of them managed to say between sniggers.

"Guess what? We let it out!" another one guffawed.

"What did you do that for?" Kirsty asked crossly.

"To make the pesky fairy pet hamster come to the rescue, of course," the third goblin replied slyly. "And when it does, we'll catch it and take it back to Jack Frost!"

Rachel frowned. "So you've set a trap for the magic hamster?" she asked. "How horrible!"

"Well, if the fairy hamster does come, we'll find it first," Kirsty said, a determined look on her face. "And we'll give it back to Harriet the Hamster Fairy!"

"No chance," shouted the first goblin. And then all three goblins disappeared, and the girls heard their big goblin feet thundering up another flight of stairs.

Kirsty groaned. "This house is so big; it's got three storeys and an attic! How are we ever going to find two little hamsters before those sneaky goblins do?"

"If there are two hamsters," Rachel reminded her. "The magic hamster might not have come to Nibbles' rescue yet."

Out of the corner of her eye, Kirsty suddenly caught a glimpse of sparkling red light in the lounge.

Curiously, she pushed the door open to see what was happening inside. "I think the magic hamster is here, Rachel," she said, her eyes wide as she gazed at the Coopers' lounge.

Both girls stood in the doorway, staring at the transformation of the room before them. The woollen rug had become a heap of wood shavings and shredded newspaper. Hamster toys were scattered everywhere, together

with a mini-maze and two large running wheels. There were even bowls of nuts and seeds standing on the floor.

"Just look!" Kirsty said. "This is hamster heaven!"

Rachel nodded. "This is definitely pet fairy magic in action," she said with a grin.

"So we'd better find the magic hamster," Kirsty pointed out, "before the goblins do!"

Rachel peeped into the mini-maze. "With a bit of luck, Nibbles will be attracted to this hamster heaven, and come scuttling in here any second," she said. "I mean, what hamster could resist all this?" As she turned to look around, her gaze fell upon the sofa and she bit her lip in excitement. "Kirsty," she said quietly, so as not to scare the little pet. "There's Nibbles!"

Kirsty looked where Rachel was pointing and saw an orange and white hamster sitting on a cushion. She stepped a little closer, to get a better look at him.

"That isn't Nibbles," she told Rachel. "Which means it must be…"

But before she could say another word, the hamster twitched its little nose and a bright shower of glittering red sparkles swirled around it. When the fairy dust cleared the girls could see a transparent plastic tube, spiralling down from the sofa to the carpet.

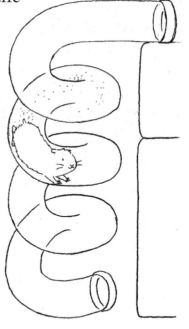

Immediately, the hamster jumped happily into the tube and started scampering down through the spiral.

Kirsty laughed. "No," she said, "that's definitely not Nibbles. It absolutely has to be the magic hamster!"

Rachel smiled as the magical pet scurried busily down through the spiral it had conjured. "I wonder if Harriet the Hamster Fairy knows her pet is here," she said excitedly.

Before Kirsty could reply, both girls heard a breathless voice cry, "Wheee!" behind them. They turned, just in time to see a big black cloud of soot billowing out from the fireplace. As the coal-dust settled, Kirsty and Rachel grinned in delight. For there on the hearth, covered from head to toe in soot, was a tiny fairy!

Twinkle, Twinkle Little Hamster

The fairy sneezed three times, blinked and then waved a sooty wand over herself. A bright stream of red sparkles shot out of the wand, whizzed around her and the soot disappeared in an instant. "That's better," she said cheerfully, and gave the girls a huge smile. "Hello, again!"

Now that she was free of soot, the
girls could see that Harriet the Hamster
Fairy was wearing a light blue dress,
tied with a darker blue sash. She wore
sparkly red shoes, and a glittery red
flower hung on a chain round her
neck, while another decorated the blue
Alice band in her short blonde hair.

"Hello, Harriet," Kirsty said, smiling at the little fairy. "We were just wondering if you were nearby."

"And here I am," Harriet said, smiling back. "I had a feeling that Twinkle, my pet, was somewhere around here."

"She is," Rachel said eagerly, "but there are three goblins too! We last saw them heading upstairs."

"Horrid things," Harriet said, fluttering up into the air, "but I'm glad Twinkle's here. Where is she?"

"She's just about to come out of that spiral tube," Kirsty said, pointing it out with a grin.

"Any second…now!"

Right on cue, Twinkle emerged. As soon as she saw Harriet, the hamster shrank to fairy pet size and scampered joyfully up into the air. Rachel and Kirsty watched in delight as the tiny magic hamster scurried towards her fairy mistress.

"Just what I was looking for!" came a gloating, goblin voice.

Rachel and Kirsty spun around in alarm to see a goblin pop up from behind the sofa with a horrible smirk on his face!

The goblin vaulted swiftly over the sofa, grabbed the tiny pet out of the air, and then rushed out of the lounge and up the stairs.

"Oh, no!" Rachel cried. "That goblin must have sneaked back downstairs looking for Twinkle. And now he's got her!"

"Quick, let's fly after him!"
Harriet suggested, waving
her wand and turning
both girls into fairies.
She zoomed out of
the door, leaving
glittering red fairy
dust shimmering
in the air behind
her, as Kirsty
and Rachel
followed using
their delicate,
shining wings.

As the three friends
flew upstairs, they
could see the goblins
standing on the next flight of
stairs that led to the upper storeys

of the house. But when they saw fairies coming towards them, the goblins turned and fled to the second floor.

"Keep going!" Harriet urged, beating her wings even faster as she zoomed ahead.

"Let's hide in here!" the girls heard a goblin shout, as they reached the top of the second flight of stairs. They were just in time to see a goblin disappearing through a doorway.

"That's Jamie's bedroom," Kirsty whispered, coming to a stop. "And it's not very big. There can't be too many hiding places in there."

"If we're girls again, it'll be easier for us to take Twinkle from the goblins," Rachel pointed out. "Could you magic us back, please, Harriet?"

"Of course," Harriet said. She waved her wand again, and sparkling red fairy dust tumbled all over Kirsty and Rachel. "There," she said, as the fairy dust worked its magic and the girls quickly grew back to their normal size.

"Now, let's go hamster hunting!"

Rachel and Kirsty crept into Jamie's bedroom, with Harriet hovering behind them. There was a bed, a wardrobe, a chest of drawers and a large toybox, but no goblins in sight.

Rachel headed straight for the toybox and lifted the lid. But there was no goblin inside, just a collection of Jamie's plastic dinosaurs, toy cars and some colourful rubber snakes.

Kirsty tiptoed over to the bed and checked under the lumpy duvet, but she didn't find a goblin underneath.

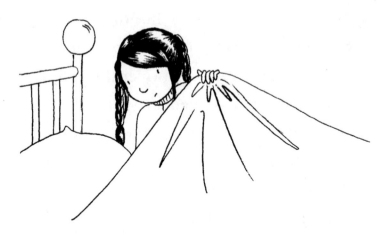

Suddenly, Harriet started fluttering around excitedly, pointing to one of the long curtains that framed the window.

The girls crept forwards to have
a closer look, and grinned at each other
excitedly; there was a distinctly
goblin-shaped bump behind the curtain!

Hamster Hide and Seek!

Kirsty and Rachel looked at each other,
both wondering what to do. Then Kirsty
had an idea. She put her finger to her
lips, warning the others to keep quiet.
She wasn't sure if the goblin behind the
curtain was the one with Twinkle or not,
but if he did have the magic hamster,
she wanted to catch him off guard.

If she could make him jump, she hoped
the goblin would loosen his grip on
Twinkle, who could then leap free!

Kirsty crept up to the curtain as
quietly as she could. Then, with a sharp
jab of her finger, she poked the curtain
right where she guessed the goblin's
tummy would be.

"Ow!" came a surprised shout.

"Caught you!"
Kirsty cried,
quickly tugging
the curtain
aside. "Now
give Twinkle
back!"

But the goblin
behind the curtain
was empty-handed.

He dodged past Kirsty and ran straight out of the bedroom.

"So that's one goblin..." Harriet mused. "Now, where are the other two?"

But even as Harriet spoke, Rachel had spotted a pair of green goblin feet sticking out from under the bed. She tiptoed back to the toybox and pulled out one of Jamie's rubber snakes. Then she winked at Kirsty and Harriet, and said in a loud voice, "Ooh! I think I just saw a snake! Do the Coopers have a pet snake too, Kirsty?"

"No," Kirsty said, guessing at Rachel's plan. "It must be a wild one. Look, there it goes, slithering under Jamie's bed! I wonder if it's poisonous…"

Trying her hardest not to giggle, Rachel pushed the rubber snake under Jamie's bed and made a loud hissing noise. Grinning cheekily, Harriet flung some red fairy dust after it, and the snake began wriggling further under the bed all by itself!

With a squeal of
alarm, the goblin
scrambled out
from his hiding
place and
rushed out of
the room. But
he wasn't holding
Twinkle either.

"That's two
goblins," sighed Harriet.
"Where could the third one be?"

Just then, the girls heard a nervous
laugh coming from inside the wardrobe.
They guessed that the third goblin must
be hiding inside it, and since the other
two didn't have Harriet's magic
hamster, this one must be the goblin
who had snatched Twinkle!

Kirsty and Rachel stood either side of the wardrobe, holding one door handle each. "One...two...three!" Rachel mouthed, then they flung open the wardrobe doors at the same time.

Kirsty's heart was pounding as she looked inside the wardrobe, ready to grab little Twinkle. But, to her dismay, there was nothing to see except lots of clothes hanging up. Had they misheard? Was the goblin somewhere else?

But sharp-eyed Harriet was pointing at something in the wardrobe and the girls saw that, there, sticking out between two of Jamie's superhero costumes, was a pointed green nose! The goblin was in the wardrobe, he was just well hidden.

Rachel spotted a Native American feathered headdress on the top shelf of the wardrobe and that gave her an idea. Kirsty and Harriet watched curiously as Rachel mimed pulling out a feather and using it to tickle the goblin's feet.

Harriet had to put a hand over her mouth to stop herself laughing at the idea. Nodding excitedly, she waved her wand over the headdress. A large red feather immediately glimmered with a sparkly light, and then leapt nimbly out of its place. The feather shot down towards the goblin's toes, where it began to tickle them all over!

"Ooh! Ahh! Ooh, stop that!" the
goblin giggled, hopping
from one foot to
another. "Ooh!
Ha ha! Stop it!
Hee hee!"

The feather went
on tickling away,
until the goblin was
breathless with laughter. Finally, he
could stand it no more. "Stop!" he
roared, between laughs. "Stop!"

"Not until you give us Twinkle!"
Rachel and Kirsty chorused firmly.

Nibbles is Nowhere

The goblin's hands appeared through the clothes at once, with a tiny, fairy pet-sized Twinkle sitting in his cupped palms. "Here – take it! Take it!" the goblin urged. "Just stop the tickling!"

Harriet flew over and scooped up Twinkle. She dropped a kiss on the hamster's little head, then waved her wand in the direction of the goblin's feet. Sparkling red fairy dust swirled around the feather, which glowed brightly once more and leapt back into its place in Jamie's headdress.

The goblin jumped out of the wardrobe and bolted through the bedroom door. "It's not fair, they were tickling me," the girls heard him moan to the other goblins.

Rachel and Kirsty
smiled at one
another, then
petted cute little
Twinkle. That
was one hamster
safe, at least!

"Now we just
have to find Nibbles,"
Rachel said. "I wonder
where he could have got to."

Twinkle was already twitching
her delicate nose and looking up at
Harriet in a meaningful way. The
fairy paid close attention, then
nodded at her pet. "Twinkle says
she senses that Nibbles is somewhere
up above us in the house," she told
Rachel and Kirsty.

"In the attic?" Kirsty said. "Wow, he's climbed a long way today!"

"Come on, let's find him right away," Rachel said, "before he goes off on another adventure!"

Kirsty, Rachel and Harriet all rushed up the last staircase to the attic door. But as soon as they stepped into the attic itself, all three of them gasped.

"Oh, no!" Kirsty cried, looking around. The small room was absolutely stuffed full of boxes and suitcases, old furniture, wooden trunks, dusty photo albums and trinkets, dimly lit by the daylight that streamed in through a tiny round window. "How are we ever going to find Nibbles in this lot?"

Luckily, Twinkle seemed to know exactly where Nibbles was. She was already scampering through the air towards a stack of travel souvenirs. Rachel could see carved wooden masks, a rather moth-eaten silk parasol, a jewellery box piled high with strings of beads, and even an old brass oil-lamp! Rachel followed Twinkle over, laughing. "I was just thinking what an Aladdin's cave it is up here," she said, "and look! There's even an Aladdin's lamp!"

Twinkle seemed interested in the lamp
too. She pushed at it with her nose,
then looked up at Harriet, her little
black eyes bright with interest.

Rachel carefully lifted the lid of the
lamp and everyone
peeped inside
curiously. There,
curled up fast
asleep, was
Nibbles!

"Oh, look!"
Rachel said,
hurriedly
dropping her
voice to a whisper
so as not to wake the
sleeping hamster. "How cute. He's
worn out after all his adventures!"

Kirsty gently scooped the sleepy hamster out of the lamp, feeling very relieved. Now all they had to do was put Nibbles back in his cage with some fresh food, and clean up the lounge. Then everything would be exactly as it should be once more.

But just as they were heading towards the door, Kirsty and Rachel heard the unmistakeable sound of goblin footsteps pounding up the attic stairs. The girls looked around quickly for some means of escape, but there was only one door and the tiny window. The goblins were coming, and the friends were trapped!

Happy Hamster

"Quick, Harriet!" Rachel cried. "Fly out of the window and take Twinkle home to Fairyland before those goblins can get their hands on her again."

"Yes," Kirsty agreed eagerly. "The goblins won't bother hanging around here once they know you and Twinkle have gone."

Harriet nodded, clutching her pet
protectively. "OK, girls. Thank you
both for all your help," she
added, zooming over to
the window. Then she
stopped on the
windowsill, as if she'd
just remembered
something. "But
before I go, I'd
better tidy up the
mess downstairs."

Her wand was
a bright blur in the air
as Harriet waved it
in a complicated pattern,
sending glittering red fairy dust
spiralling out of the door. "There!" she
said, sounding pleased with herself.

"And thank you again, girls," she added, hugging them goodbye. "You've both been brilliant!"

"Goodbye Harriet. Goodbye Twinkle," Rachel and Kirsty said quickly, because the goblin footsteps were growing nearer by the second!

Harriet fluttered out through the open window, just as the three goblins clattered into the attic.

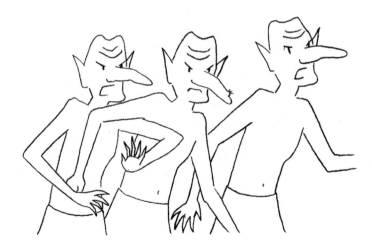

"After that fairy!" the first goblin
shouted, seeing the last traces of fairy
magic glimmering round the window.

"She's outside. Quick, let's follow her,"
the second one shouted, turning around
so fast that he bumped straight into the
third goblin.

"Hey! Watch where you're going!"
snapped the third goblin, turning to
hurry back down the attic stairs.

"Well, it's your fault that the hamster got away," Kirsty and Rachel heard one of the other goblins telling him as they all stomped away.

"My fault! How do you work that out?" came the indignant reply, drifting faintly up the stairs.

The goblins were soon out of earshot, so Rachel and Kirsty ran over to the attic window to see if they could spot them in the garden. Moments later, they saw the three goblins appear outside, bickering noisily about which way Harriet had gone.

A sparrow suddenly flew across the garden, and one of the goblins pointed excitedly at it. "There's the fairy!" he shouted. And the silly goblins chased eagerly after the sparrow as it darted over the back fence and into the meadow behind the Coopers' garden.

Meanwhile, on Kirsty's hand, Nibbles opened his eyes and gazed around as if he was surprised to find himself there.

"Hello, Nibbles," Kirsty said, stroking him. "Let's get you something to eat. What an adventure you've had!"

The girls headed back downstairs and saw that Harriet had worked her wonderful fairy magic, as promised; the lounge was spotless.

"Wow!" said Rachel, with a grin. "You'd never guess that this room was full of wood shavings and hamster toys just a few minutes ago!"

Kirsty put Nibbles back into his cage and couldn't help smiling.

Harriet hadn't just taken care of the
messy lounge, she'd also magically filled
up Nibbles' bowl with a large helping
of sunflower seeds! "His favourite food,"
Kirsty said, watching the hamster tuck
in hungrily. "Clever Harriet!"

Kirsty carefully shut the
cage door and looked
at the happy little
hamster for a few
moments. "You
know, I think I'll
take Nibbles back
to my house with
us," she said. "Just so
that we know for sure he's
safe from any goblin mischief."

"Good idea," Rachel said. "Then
Nibbles will get a little holiday, too."

Kirsty wrote a note
to Jamie, telling him
where Nibbles was,
and left it on the
table in the lounge.
Then she carefully
carried the hamster
cage over to the door.

"Phew," Rachel sighed, as she and
Kirsty left the Coopers' house. "That was
a busy morning!" She smiled at her friend.
"What could possibly happen tomorrow?"

Kirsty grinned. "I don't know," she
replied happily. "But I can't wait to
find out!"

Win a Rainbow Magic
Sparkly T-Shirt and Goody Bag!

In every book in the Rainbow Magic Pet Keeper Fairies
series (books 29-35) there is a hidden picture of a collar
with a secret letter in it. Find all seven letters and
re-arrange them to make a special Fairyland word,
then send it to us. Each month we will put the entries
into a draw and select one winner to receive
a Rainbow Magic Sparkly T-shirt and Goody Bag!

Send your entry on a postcard to Rainbow Magic Pet
Keeper Competition, Orchard Books, 338 Euston Road,
London NW1 3BH. Australian readers should
write to Hachette Children's Books, Level 17/207
Kent Street, Sydney, NSW 2000.
Don't forget to include your name and address.
Only one entry per child. Final draw: 30th April 2007.

Don't miss...
Kylie the Carnival Fairy

1-84616-175-4

Kylie the Carnival Fairy needs Kirsty's and Rachel's help! Jack Frost has stolen the three magic hats that make the Sunnydays Carnival so much fun, and the girls have to get them back...

Have you checked out the

website at:

www.rainbowmagic.co.uk

There are games, activities and fun things to do, as well as news and information about Rainbow Magic and all of the fairies.

by Daisy Meadows

The Rainbow Fairies

Ruby the Red Fairy	ISBN	1 84362 016 2
Amber the Orange Fairy	ISBN	1 84362 017 0
Saffron the Yellow Fairy	ISBN	1 84362 018 9
Fern the Green Fairy	ISBN	1 84362 019 7
Sky the Blue Fairy	ISBN	1 84362 020 0
Izzy the Indigo Fairy	ISBN	1 84362 021 9
Heather the Violet Fairy	ISBN	1 84362 022 7

The Weather Fairies

Crystal the Snow Fairy	ISBN	1 84362 633 0
Abigail the Breeze Fairy	ISBN	1 84362 634 9
Pearl the Cloud Fairy	ISBN	1 84362 635 7
Goldie the Sunshine Fairy	ISBN	1 84362 641 1
Evie the Mist Fairy	ISBN	1 84362 636 5
Storm the Lightning Fairy	ISBN	1 84362 637 3
Hayley the Rain Fairy	ISBN	1 84362 638 1

The Party Fairies

Cherry the Cake Fairy	ISBN	1 84362 818 X
Melodie the Music Fairy	ISBN	1 84362 819 8
Grace the Glitter Fairy	ISBN	1 84362 820 1
Honey the Sweet Fairy	ISBN	1 84362 821 X
Polly the Party Fun Fairy	ISBN	1 84362 822 8
Phoebe the Fashion Fairy	ISBN	1 84362 823 6
Jasmine the Present Fairy	ISBN	1 84362 824 4

The Jewel Fairies

The Pet Keeper Fairies

All priced at £3.99. *Holly the Christmas Fairy, Summer the Holiday Fairy,
Stella the Star Fairy* and *Kylie the Carnival Fairy* are priced at £4.99.
The Rainbow Magic Treasury is priced at £12.99.
Rainbow Magic books are available from all good bookshops, or can be ordered
direct from the publisher: Orchard Books, PO BOX 29, Douglas IM99 1BQ
Credit card orders please telephone 01624 836000
or fax 01624 837033 or visit our Internet site: www.wattspub.co.uk
or e-mail: bookshop@enterprise.net for details.

To order please quote title, author and ISBN and your full name and address.
Cheques and postal orders should be made payable to 'Bookpost plc.'
Postage and packing is FREE within the UK
(overseas customers should add £2.00 per book).
Prices and availability are subject to change.

Look out for the Fun Day Fairies!

MEGAN THE MONDAY FAIRY
1-84616-188-6

TALLULAH THE TUESDAY FAIRY
1-84616-189-4

WILLOW THE WEDNESDAY FAIRY
1-84616-190-8

THEA THE THURSDAY FAIRY
1-84616-191-6

FREYA THE FRIDAY FAIRY
1-84616-192-4

SIENNA THE SATURDAY FAIRY
1-84616-193-2

SARAH THE SUNDAY FAIRY
1-84616-194-0

Available from
Saturday 2nd September 2006